Dear Parent:
Your child's love of reading starts here!

Every child learns to read in a different way and at his or her own speed. Some go back and forth between reading levels and read favorite books again and again. Others read through each level in order. You can help your young reader improve and become more confident by encouraging his or her own interests and abilities. From books your child reads with you to the first books he or she reads alone, there are I Can Read Books for every stage of reading:

SHARED READING
Basic language, word repetition, and whimsical illustrations, ideal for sharing with your emergent reader

BEGINNING READING
Short sentences, familiar words, and simple concepts for children eager to read on their own

READING WITH HELP
Engaging stories, longer sentences, and language play for developing readers

READING ALONE
Complex plots, challenging vocabulary, and high-interest topics for the independent reader

ADVANCED READING
Short paragraphs, chapters, and exciting themes for the perfect bridge to chapter books

I Can Read Books have introduced children to the joy of reading since 1957. Featuring award-winning authors and illustrators and a fabulous cast of beloved characters, I Can Read Books set the standard for beginning readers.

A lifetime of discovery begins with the magical words "I Can Read!"

Visit www.icanread.com for information
on enriching your child's reading experience.

Superman: Superman Versus Bizarro
SUPERMAN and all related characters and elements are trademarks of DC Comics © 2010. All rights reserved.
Manufactured in U.S.A. No part of this book may be used or reproduced in any manner whatsoever without written permission except in the case of brief quotations embodied in critical articles and reviews. For information address HarperCollins Children's Books, a division of HarperCollins Publishers, 195 Broadway, New York, NY 10007.
www.icanread.com

Library of Congress catalog card number: 2009930271
ISBN 978-0-06-188516-7
Book design by John Sazaklis

16 17 18 19 20   LSCC   10   ❖   First Edition

I Can Read!

READING 2 WITH HELP

SUPERMAN

Superman
Versus Bizarro

by Chris Strathearn
pictures by MADA Design, Inc.

SUPERMAN created by Jerry Siegel and Joe Shuster

HARPER
An Imprint of HarperCollinsPublishers

CLARK KENT

Clark Kent
lives in Metropolis.
He is secretly Superman.

LOIS LANE

Lois Lane is a
newspaper reporter.
She writes a lot
about Superman.

BIZARRO

Bizarro looks
a lot like Superman,
but he has opposite powers.

SUPERMAN

Superman has many amazing powers.
He was born on the planet Krypton.

BIZARRO WORLD

Bizarro comes from a
planet called Bizarro World.
It is a lot like Earth, except
that everything is backward.

One morning in Metropolis,
Clark Kent was walking to work.
The streets were crowded and noisy
with the sounds of cars and people.
Clark heard something else.

Clark could hear a scared cat
cry from far away.
Clark stepped into an alley
and changed into his costume.
"This is a job for Superman!"

The cat was stuck high in a tree.

Superman swooped down to help,

but someone was already there!

Under the tree was a strange man.

It was Superman's backward clone!

His name was Bizarro.

"The kitty is scaring the tree!"

shouted Bizarro.

"Bizarro must save the tree!"

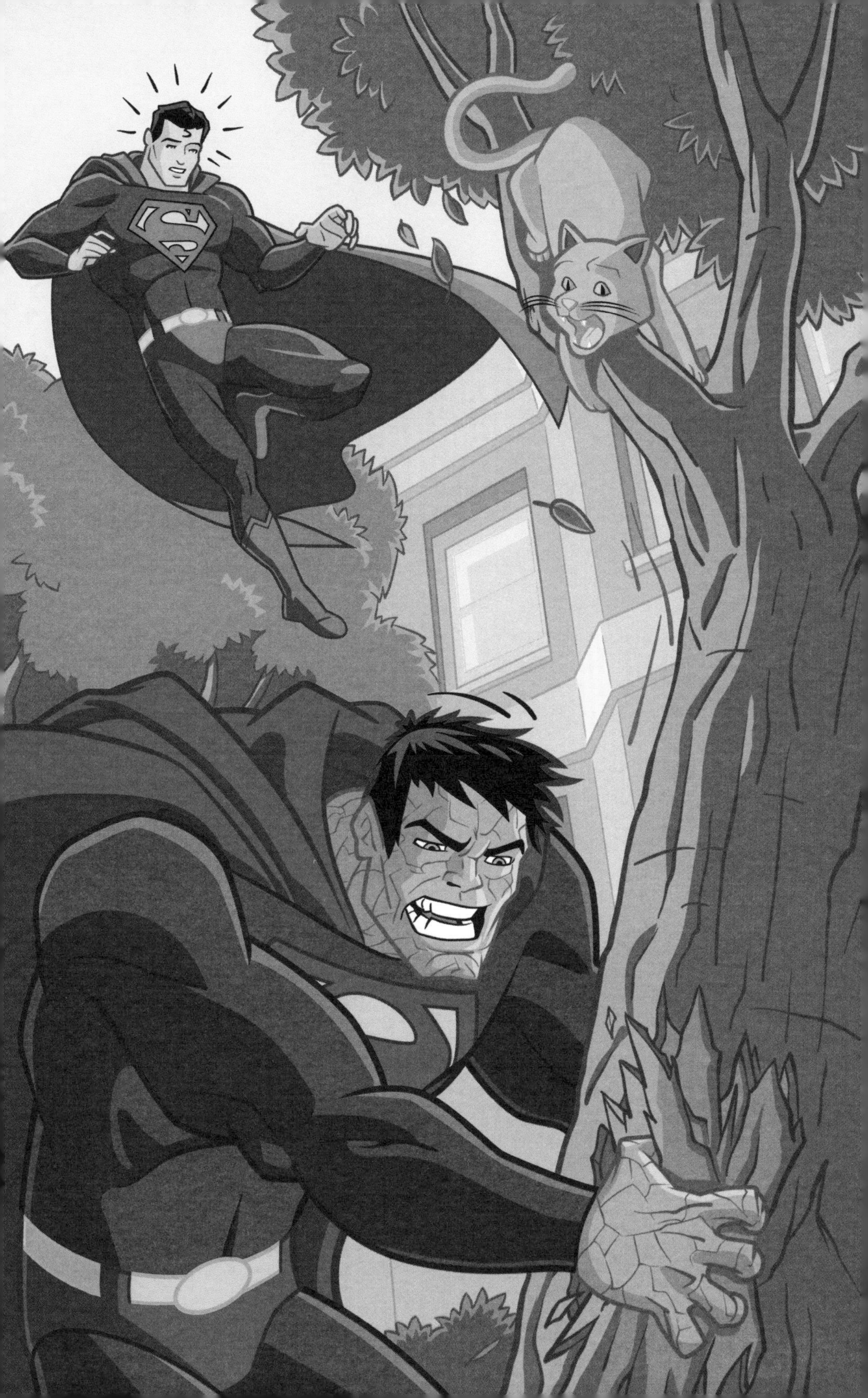

Bizarro grabbed the tree trunk

and pulled it from the ground.

CRASH!

Bizarro was powerful but clumsy.

"Bizarro is the best hero!"

said Bizarro as he flew off.

"I should follow him to make sure

he won't save anything else!"

said Superman.

Superman followed Bizarro

all the way to a burning warehouse.

"Bizarro will help the firemen!"

said Bizarro.

Bizarro lifted a fire truck over his head.

"Fire trucks put out fires!" he said.

"Wait!" said Superman.

Bizarro didn't wait.

He tossed the truck at the fire.

It crashed and exploded!

"Done!" said Bizarro.

Once again, Bizarro flew away,
but the fire was still burning!
Superman quickly blew out the flames
with jets of icy air.

"Does Bizarro think he's a hero?"

Lois Lane asked Superman

after he put out the fire.

"Yes," said Superman,

"but his thinking is backward

because he is from Bizarro World.

Bizarro must return to his own planet."

"Please make him leave before

he destroys Metropolis!" Lois said.

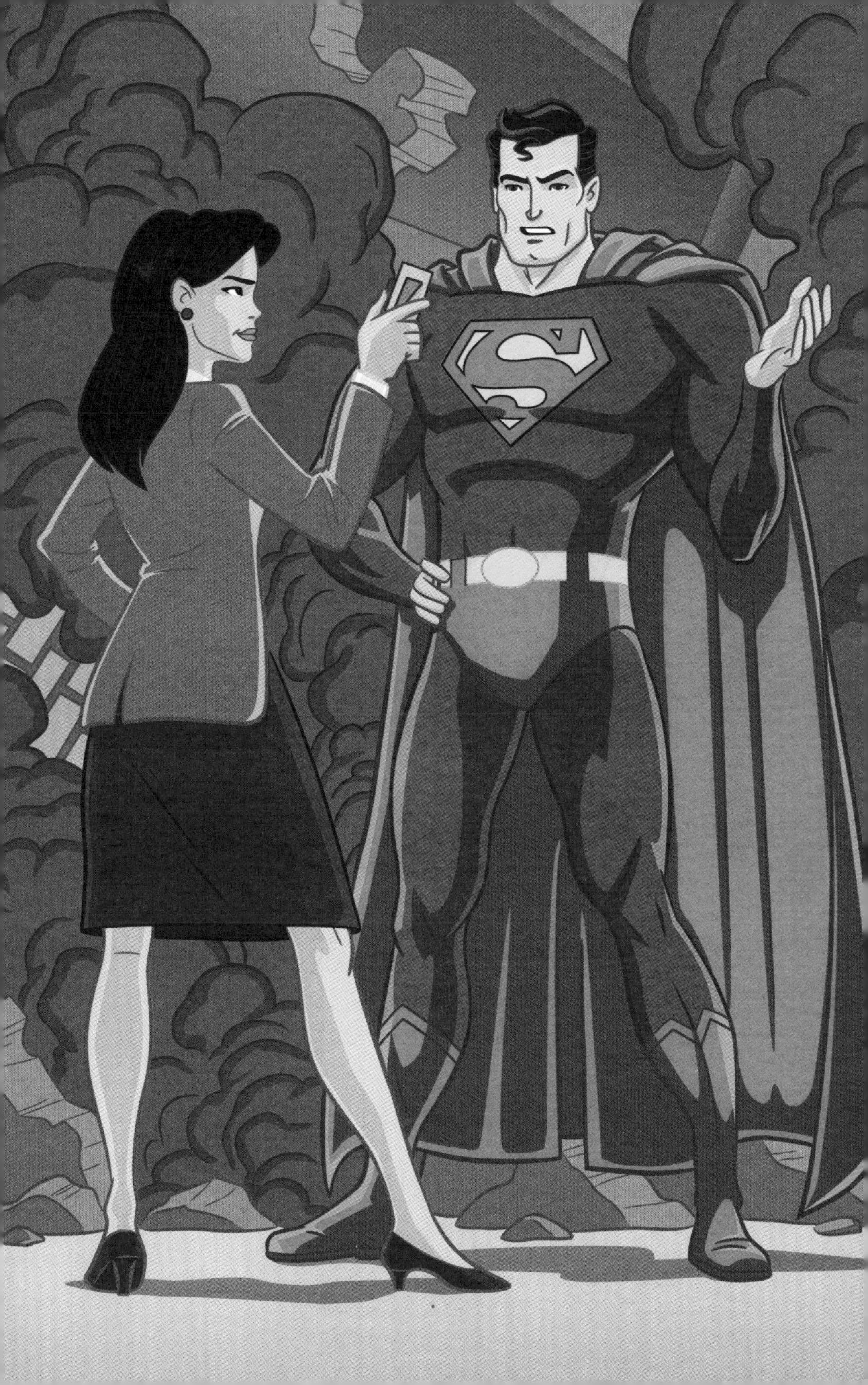

Superman heard new cries for help.

A boat was sinking in the river.

There was no time to lose.

Superman had to get there before Bizarro!

Bizarro was already at the boat.

"No problem!" said Bizarro.

"The river is hurting the boat,
so Bizarro will stop the river!"

Bizarro knocked down a bridge.

CRASH! SPLASH! WHOOSH!

Pieces of rock and steel

piled up high in the river.

Superman picked up the boat
and flew it to safety.

Now the river was overflowing.

It was going to flood the city!

With super-speed and super-strength,
Superman moved the rocks and steel
that blocked the river.
Water began to flow once more.
"Now to rebuild the bridge!" he said.

Superman used his heat rays
to weld the bridge back together.
Bizarro was angry at Superman.
"What are you doing?" he yelled.

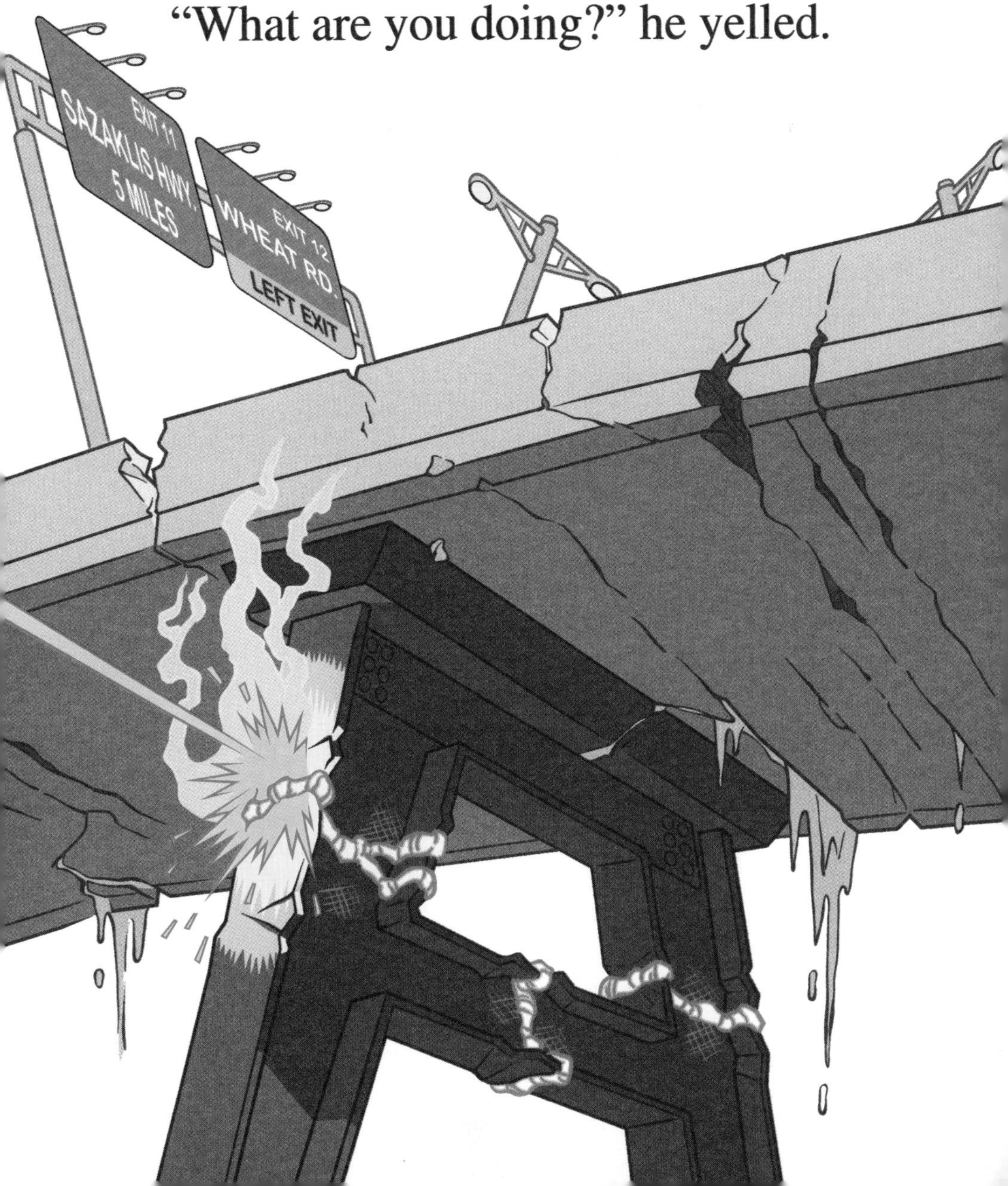
EXIT 11
SAZAKLIS HWY.
5 MILES
EXIT 12
WHEAT RD.
LEFT EXIT

"Bizarro is the hero,

not Superman!" Bizarro yelled.

Superman faced Bizarro.

"Bizarro, you can't stay on Earth!

It's time for you to go home!"

Bizarro stomped his feet.

The ground trembled and shook.

"No!" he shouted.

"Superman should leave Metropolis!"

Bizarro threw a statue at Superman.

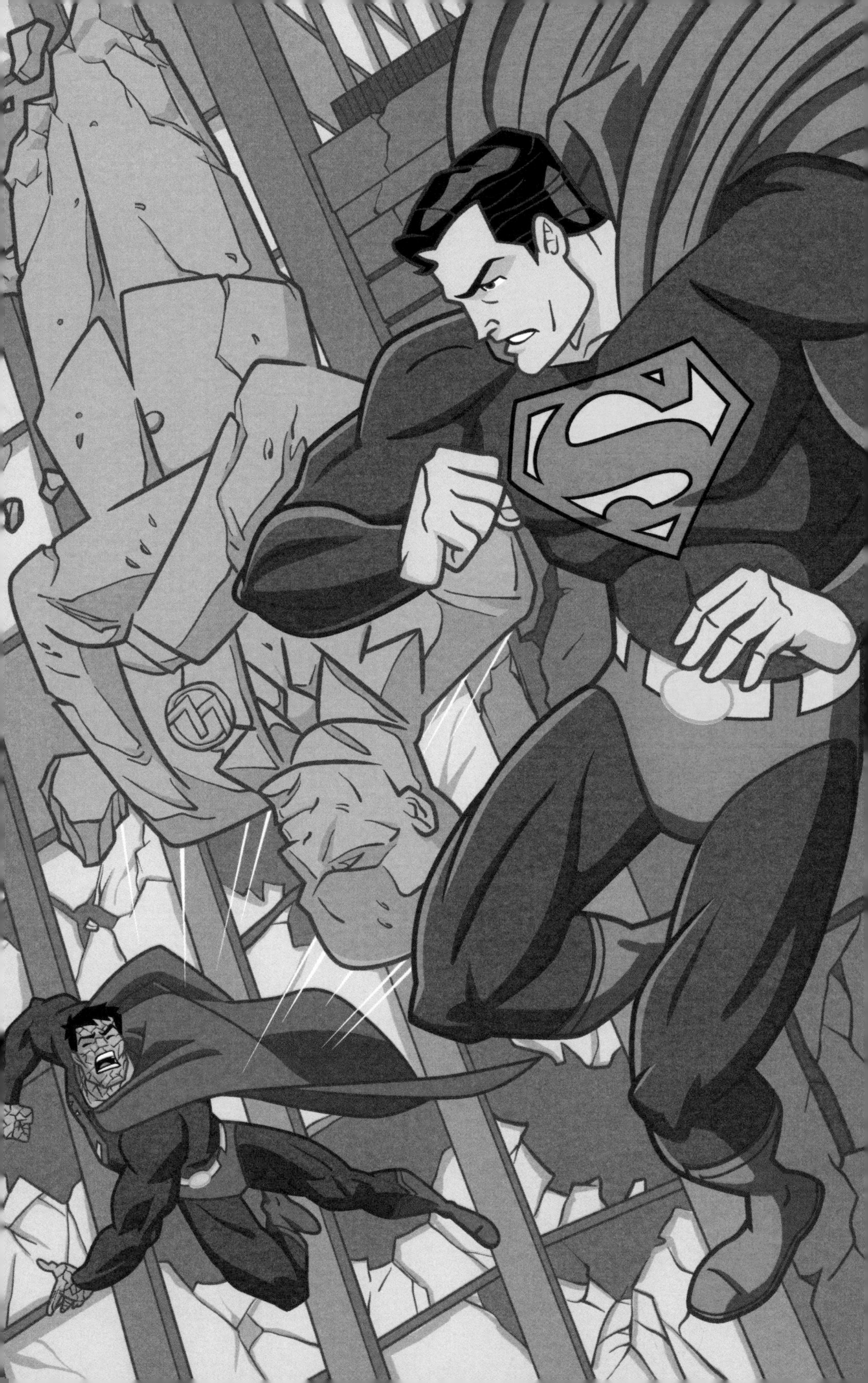

Superman dodged the statue,

but Bizarro attacked again.

He shot freeze rays from his eyes.

Superman was covered in ice.

"Ha!" laughed Bizarro.

"Superman is not so hot anymore!"

Superman easily broke free.

"Bizarro, look around you!"
Superman pointed at the mess.
"You can't fix anything on Earth.
Your backward thinking is good
only on Bizarro World!"

Bizarro suddenly grew quiet.

He knew Superman was right.

"Bizarro is tired of Earth, anyway.

It is too backward here," he said.

"If I'm needed here," said Superman,

"you must be needed on your world."

This cheered Bizarro up.

"Bizarro is a big hero over there!"

he said proudly.

Bizarro turned and flew away.

He left Earth for Bizarro World

and the Bizarro people who needed him.

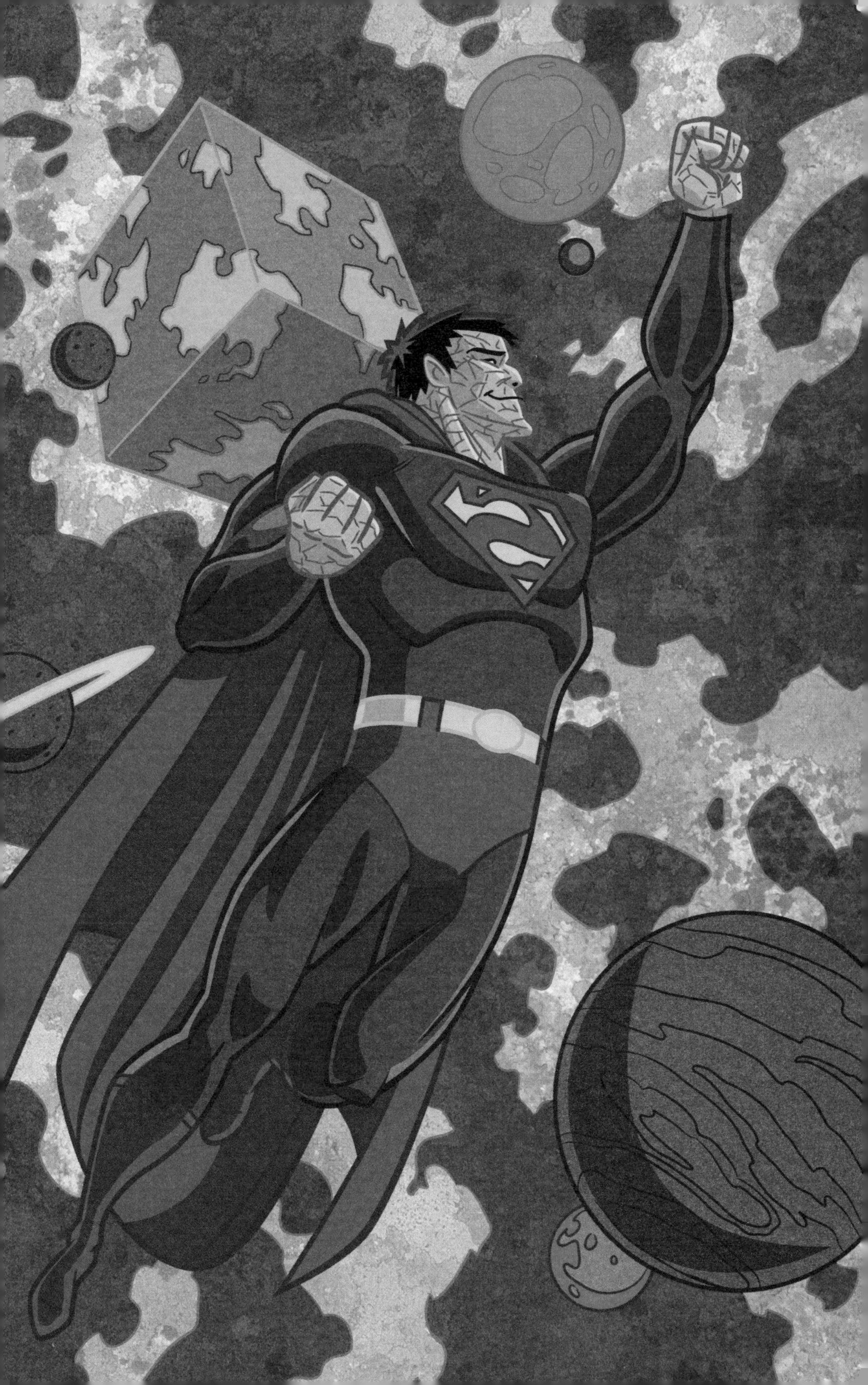

Back on Bizarro World,
a woman cried out.
"Help! Kitty is hurting the tree!"
Bizarro knew just what to do.

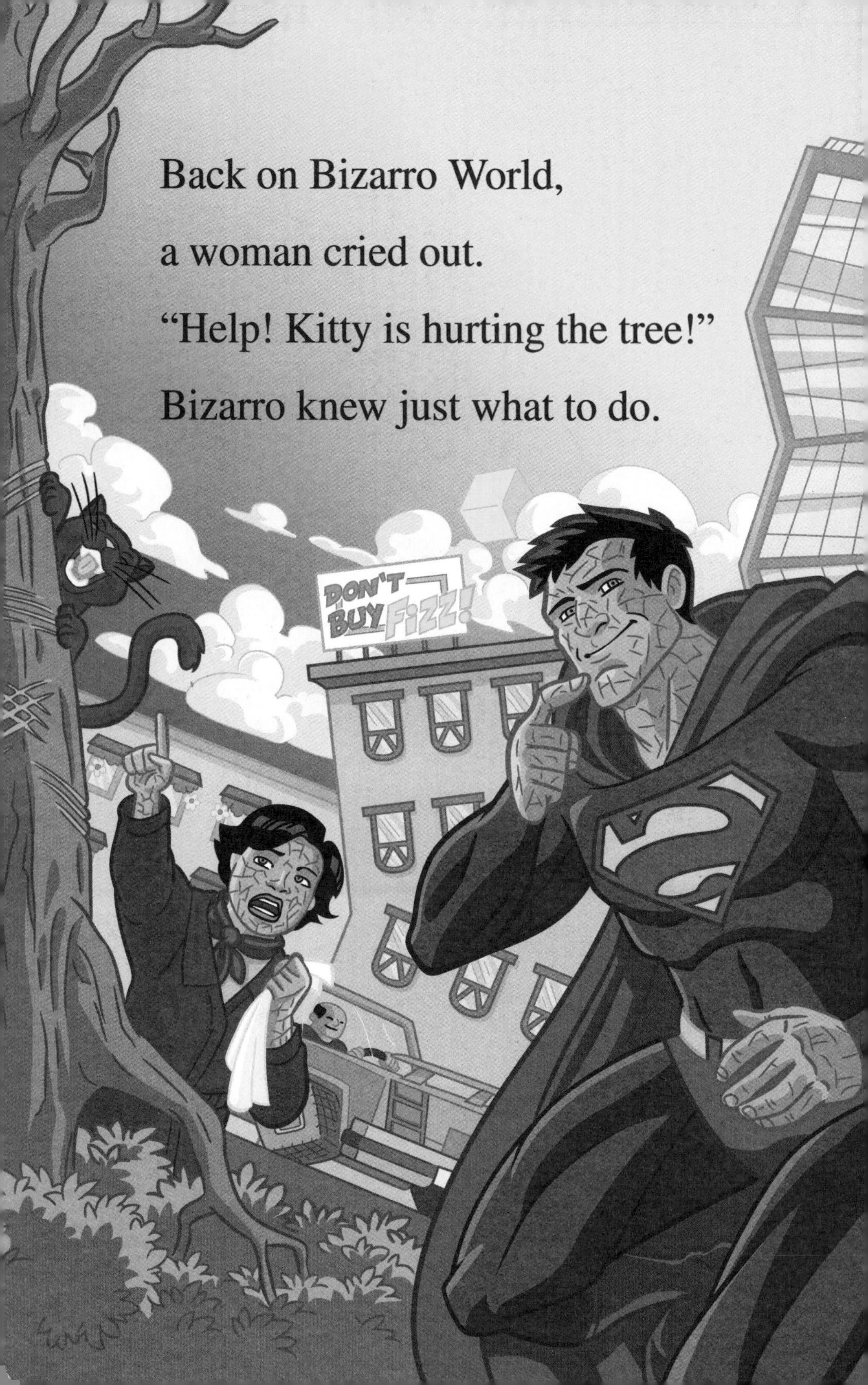
DON'T BUY FIZZ!